GARY CHALK'S

Hide & Seek in History

A DK PUBLISHING BOOK

First American Edition, 1997
2 4 6 8 10 9 7 5 3 1

Published in the United States by
DK Publishing, Inc.
95 Madison Avenue
New York, New York 10016

Visit us on the World Wide Web at http://www.dk.com

Published in Great Britain by Dorling Kindersley Ltd.

A catalog record is
available from the Library of Congress.

ISBN 0-7894-1500-3

Reproduced by DOT Gradations
Printed and bound by Partenaires, France

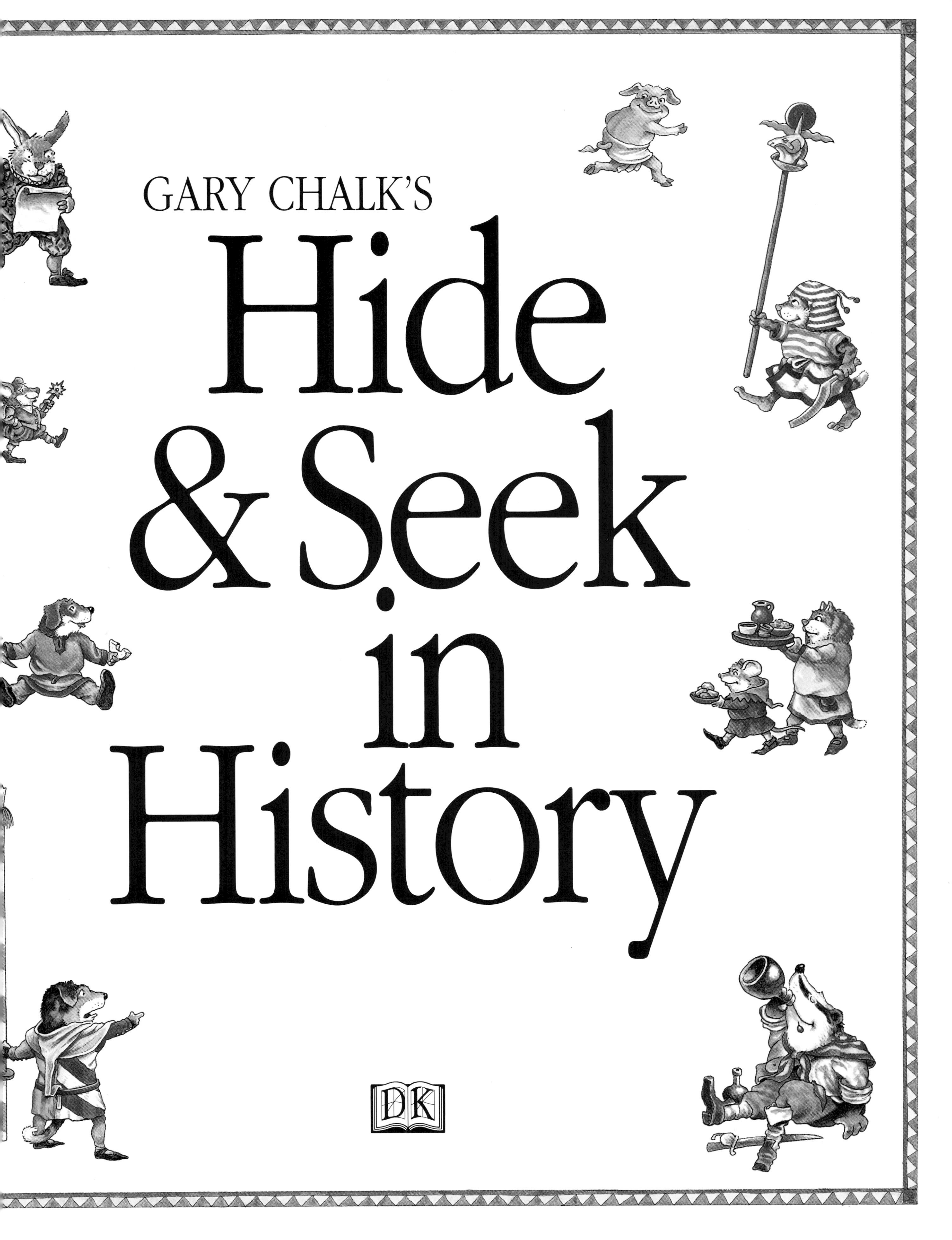

GARY CHALK'S

Hide & Seek in History

DK

The Scavengers

Once upon the future, in a land at the end of time, you will find a junk store owned by three Scavengers. Traveling in their time machine to historic times and places, they hunt for interesting articles to sell. They always choose the busiest places, where they won't be noticed.

Can you spot the Scavengers in each historic scene?

•

Look in the junk store on page 22.
What did the Scavengers take from each scene?

Honey detector

Matter-disrupter can bore holes through the thickest walls.

Hold-all bag for tools

Otto

Umbrella end can be used to pick locks.

The Scavengers can send each other phone and video messages via their mini-communicators.

Polly

Telescope

Dynamite can blast obstacles.

Snib

These items are especially well hidden. Can you find them? Did the Scavengers find them, too? (Look on page 22.)

Egyptian toy hippopotamus

Roman purse

Viking shield

Medieval jester's rattle

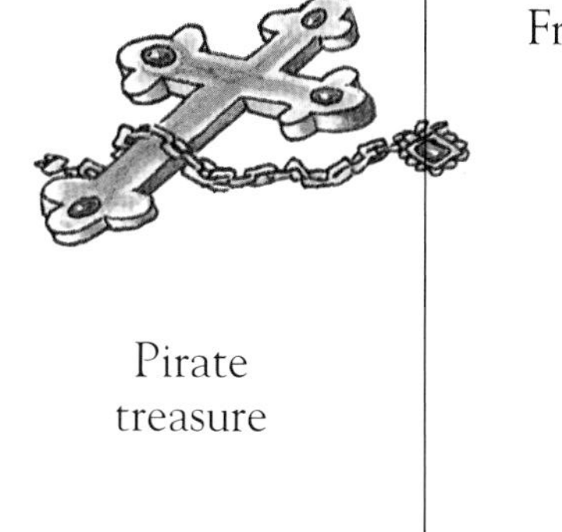

Elizabethan theater prop

Pirate treasure

French teapot

Wild West drinking bottle

The Time Machine

Otto built the Scavengers' time machine out of pieces of junk. It contains lots of pods that can be attached to the back for carrying more junk.

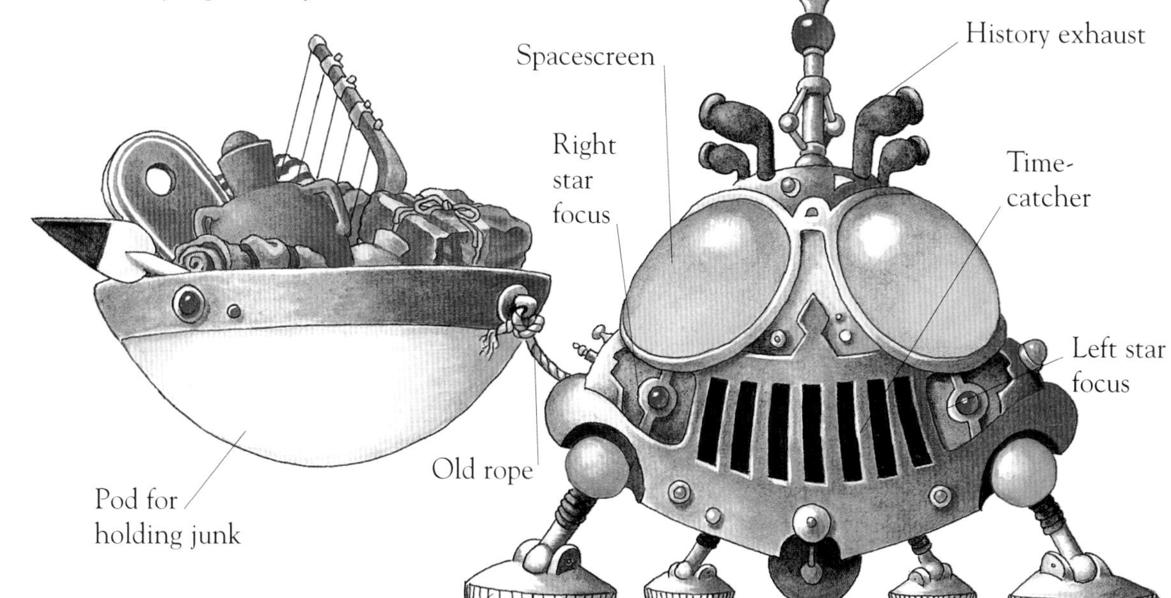

Travel Schedule

ON THE BANKS OF THE NILE

The Scavengers start their journey in ancient Egypt. While Pharaoh relaxes with music in his palace, the busy banks of the Nile hum with activity. There's no time to visit the pyramids, but there's plenty of treasure in the wealthiest country in the ancient world.

FUN AND GAMES

Egyptians enjoyed lively music, song, and dance.

Children played with balls, dolls, and wooden toys shaped like animals.

Egyptians wore makeup, wigs, and jewelry. Cones of perfumed fat on their wigs made them smell nice.

WORK 6

Farmers harvested crops of wheat and barley with sickles.

Scribes wrote on sheets of papyrus using a reed pen.

Soldiers carried painted wooden shields and sharp spears for protection.

Teams of oarsmen rowed ceremonial barges owned by rich Egyptians.

Merchants traded crops for gold and luxuries.

cargo will make me rich."
"I'll trade this linen for jewelry."
"Hold tight!"
"Glug, glug."
spears look sharp."
"Good point."
"Will someone help me raise the sail?"
"What shall I inscribe?"
"Single file up the Nile!"
"It's hot weather for marching."
"I hate doing the cleaning up."
"Not for a few more years."
"Is the new pyramid nearly finished?"
"I hope he's had his lunch."
"Just one sip."
"Yum!"
"I saw that coming."
"Sorry to barge in."
"Ssh! The princess is napping…"
"I hope he can doggie paddle."
"Oops!"
"Zzz…"
"Isn't the Nile wide enough for both of us?"
"This is a brand new barge!"
"Learn how to steer!"
"My royal wig fell in the river."
"I'll make a splash in my new kilt."
1000 BC
0
AD 1000
AD 1600
AD 1700
AD 1800

Ancient Rome

In the Roman arena the gladiators are fighting fiercely. The crowd is going wild over the cruel show, and so is the emperor. No one will notice the Scavengers.

"Peek-a-boo, I see you!"
"I'm good with the knife."
"I prefer a fork."
"I could run faster without this armor."
"You can't escape the net!"
"Go back and fight!"
"The crowd doesn't like cowards."
"I can't watch anymore . . ."
"Pass the olives."
"Here's two denarii."
"Thumbs down, Brutus, you're history!"
"Pay up. Your man's lost."
"I won my bet!"
1000 BC
0
AD 1000
AD 1600
AD 1700
AD 1800

Viking Village

It's all hustle and bustle in the Scandinavian Viking village. The new warship is nearly finished, and traders from far and wide are selling their wares. Has one of them got something for the Scavengers?

Viking Odds and Ends

Terrifying beasts were carved onto ships' prows to scare enemies.

A warrior's ax and spear were his most prized possessions.

The board game "hneftafl" was very popular.

Viking Characters

The blacksmith made iron weapons and tools in the forge.

Viking children didn't go to school – they helped out in the house and on the farm.

Viking traders traveled east, helping found a state in the Ukraine.

Arabs came north to trade with the Vikings.

Furriers sold ermine and mink from Siberia.

Vikings preserved fish and meat by salting it and hanging it out to dry.
"He's the apple of his mother's eye."
"Thwack!"
"Hee! Hee!"
"That'll teach you."
"I see you've got an ax to grind."
"Blow me down, it's hot in here."
Slaves, or thralls, fetched and carried for their masters.
Spun wool to be made into clothing was wound around a board.
"It's the latest model."
"I'm not enthralled by this."
Longhorn cows were raised for their milk and meat.
"Lucky he likes heavy metal."
"Bjorn's new chain mail weighs a ton."
"Onion makes your breath smell."
Viking traders went to Arab lands to exchange timber and iron for beautiful silks.
"Fur coats for the ladies."
"Who will buy this genuine Arab pot?"
"Ooh, she never did."
"Honk."
"How much?"
"I wish he'd lose some weight."
"I remember when . . ."
"I'm bored with this game."
"It's my turn, you cheat."
"I'd better fetch some more hay for the roof."
"Have you got one in blue?"
"Mom, Mom, can I have one?"
1000 BC
0
AD 1000
AD 1600
AD 1700
AD 1800

CASTLE TOURNAMENT

The king is holding a joust on the castle grounds. There's a carnival atmosphere – the ladies are in their best finery and the knights in their armor. Only the servants are working. How will the Scavengers find their way around without being spotted?

THE KING AND HIS KNIGHTS

In a joust, a knight tried to knock his opponent off his horse with a long lance.

A lady wore the colors of her favorite knight.

The knight's squire held up his master's flag.

SERVANTS AND PEASANTS

Lookouts were badly paid, so they didn't always concentrate on the job.

The king's secretary, often a monk, wrote out everything

"Well, he's never going to notice."
The king wore his crown and scepter on special occasions.
"What should I write about today?"
"My lady's sure to be in a spin."
"Sir Lance-a-lot's been knocked off his horse again."
"Check, mate!"
"She's supposed to be watering the garden."
"Pigeon pie again tonight."
"Keep your paws off me!"
Ladies-in-waiting spun and wove clothes for the royal family.
"Tweet!"
Court jesters made everyone laugh. They carried around a pig's bladder, which rattled.
"More firewood?"
"What a job!"
"Time for me to make an entrance."
"I wish I was old enough to joust!"
"I can hear bagpipes – I must be dreaming."
Peasants did jobs around the castle in return for protection from the king.
The "gong farmer" shoveled up after everyone.
"We have to keep the swords sharp."
"What a grind."
"I only just swept up the yard!"
"Pipe down, you windbag!"
Prisoners were often left to rot in the dungeon.
1000 BC
0
AD 1000
AD 1600
AD 1700
AD 1800

AT THE THEATER

It's showtime at the Globe theater in London. The crowds are arriving to watch the latest play. The Scavengers want to get the best view in the house.

ACTORS AND STAGEHANDS

The tiremaster took care of the costumes, which were second-hand clothes.

Boys were dressed as girls to play female parts – there were no female actors. A padded "bum" roll was worn under a skirt to give an actor a woman's hips.

Actors made surprise entrances through the trapdoor.

THE AUDIENCE

"Groundlings" paid a penny to stand in the yard in front of the stage. They were always very noisy.

Rich people paid up to three pennies to sit in the covered gallery.

Food vendors sold members of the audience ale, nuts, and fruit to snack on during the play.

Props were always the actual thing. Actors used real weapons in fight scenes.
"This is just as interesting as the show inside."
"Is this a comedy or a tragedy?"
"It's a hide-and-seek history."
Buskers performed outside the theater for hours before the play. Theater-goers arrived early to save seats for themselves and their friends.
"That'll be one penny to stand or three to sit."
"On balance, it's a dog's life."
"How long can I keep them all in the air?"
"Whatever you're selling, I'll buy some."
"His stilts look wobbly."
"Shall I watch the acrobats, the jugglers, or the play?"
1000 BC
0
AD 1000
AD 1600
AD 1700
AD 1800

Pirates Ahoy!

A dastardly pirate crew is attacking a town in the Caribbean. Soldiers are defending it. The pirates are carrying off the town treasure. What will be left for the Scavengers?

The pirate captain had to be even fiercer than his crew to keep control.

A pirate's favorite weapon was a curved, wide-handled sword called a cutlass.

The skull and cross-bones on the Jolly Roger flag warned pirates' victims to surrender without a fight.

Treasure was piled on the quay to be shared out equally among the pirates after the battle.

Flintlock pistols were loaded with black powder, kept in a flask worn around the waist.

Officers carried spontoons, or long spears, to prod their men into line.

Pirates wore a gold earring because they thought it improved their eyesight.

Grenadiers threw grenades, lit by burning pieces of string.

Artillery officers in charge of cannons spied enemy ships through "bring 'em nears," or telescopes.

Water was kept in huge, earthenware jugs to keep it cool in the Caribbean sun.

The French Revolution

The French peasants don't want to work for the rich aristocrats any more. They can't afford to buy bread, and they want their fair share of things. They start a revolution that changes the world. The Scavengers are grabbing their share, too.

The Aristocrats

The aristocrats lived in big houses and wore luxurious clothes.

They desperately wanted to hang on to their property and power.

The Revolutionaries

Revolutionaries wrote pamphlets and made speeches about their ideas.

The Revolution was a chance for the poor to punish the rich.

Revolutionaries wore the red cap of liberty,

and the blue, white, and red tricolor, colors of the new French Republic.

The peasants raided army quarters and shops for weapons,

The aristocrats wore powdered wigs. They were no longer fashionable after the Revolution.
"Excuse my table manners."
"Where's the bread?"
The revolutionaries destroyed the records of the rich. If no one could prove who owned property, peasants could claim it for themselves.
"Grab the silver."
"I'd rather eat cake."
"I've been framed."
"Down with the enemies of liberty and equality."
"Do I hear someone at the door?"
"I'd better take to my heels."
"Now they are called to account."
"Let's Blast the Past!"
or used their own scythes and pitchforks.
"That's us!"
"This property belongs to the nation."
"Revolution is war!"
"I don't like violence."
"Tremble, tyrants, your time has come!"
1000 BC
0
AD 1000
AD 1600
AD 1700
AD 1800

THE WILD WEST

"There's gold in them thar hills," and the Scavengers have joined the rush to the American West. The West is "Wild" because it is full of outlaws. If the Scavengers find treasure, will they be able to hang on to it?

THE MINERS

Prospectors came to the West from all over the world to look for gold and silver.

Many trees had to be chopped down in order to clear space for the mines.

Canaries in cages were taken down in the mines to test the air quality. If they lived, it showed the air was safe to breathe.

The underground mine was made by blasting holes in the rock with dynamite.
THE TOWN
Cattle were herded across the West. There were many fights over who owned them.
Cow towns and mining settlements weren't pleasant for females.
Outlaws on horseback robbed banks and rustled, or stole, cattle.
"Hope he's got a long fuse."
"Get ready for a big bang, everybody."
"I'm sure I can hear something through this rock."
"It's tough working by candlelight."
BARBER
Shaves • Haircuts
GENERAL STORE
"Holy cow! It's a shoot-out."
"Lock up your valuables. The outlaws are back."
"We'll be back!"
"Dance, Tender Foot!"
"This town has no appreciation of painting."
"The sheriff is taking a nap."
"Bless my soul! It's Billy the Kid."
"This town is going to need a doctor."
"Yeah. The gold in my saddlebag is mighty heavy."
"I thought it would be fun to be a cowboy!"
"Let's stop horsing around and get outta here."
1000 BC
0
AD 1000
AD 1600
AD 1700
AD 1800

THE SCAVENGERS' JUNK STORE

The Scavengers finish their journey back in the future, in the land at the end of time. They park the time machine next to the junk store, unload the pods, then open their doors to all kinds of customers.

Did they find the articles shown on page 4? What else did they scavenge?

Brainwaves are communicated through electronic hats.

Shoppers wear magnifying glasses to examine the small details of articles.

Spaceboards cause all kinds of trouble, but they are the coolest way to travel.

Hoverbugs are the fastest kind of interplanetary transportation.

Telebuttons flash when a message is sent to a mini-communicator.

"Twentieth-century antiques now on sale!"

Dodos scavenged on previous trips are sold as pets.

Cleaners have to balance carefully on floating minipods.

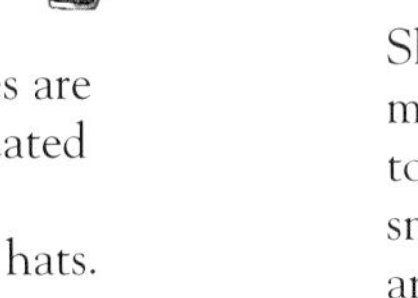

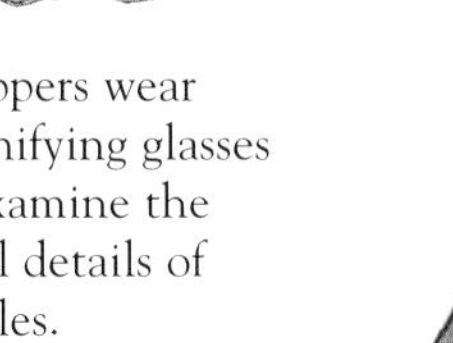

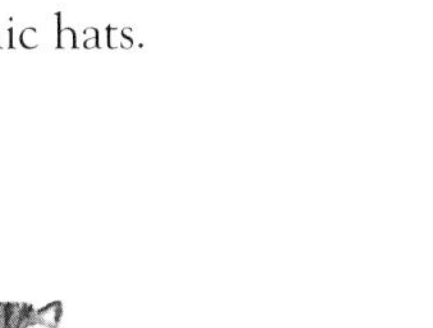

Space juice cools you down after a hard day's shopping.

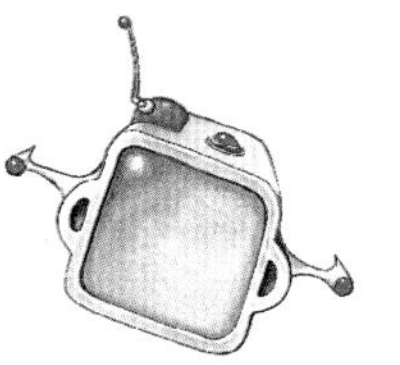

A flying monitor keeps an eye on traffic.

Computer locks recognize regular customers and open the store doors to let them in.

Time wand tells the shopper the date an article was made.

Ufones blare out messages about the latest bargains.